THE
CAT'S BATON
IS GONE

THE CAT'S BATON

Written by
Scott Hennesy

Concept and Pictures by
Joe Lanzisero

IS GONE 🎵

A Musical CAT-tastrophe

Disney • HYPERION BOOKS • NEW YORK

First Edition
10 9 8 7 6 5 4 3 2
H106-9333-5-13158
Reinforced binding
Printed in Malaysia

Library of Congress Cataloging-in-Publication Data
Hennesy, Scott.
The cat's baton is gone : a musical cat-tastrophe / by Scott Hennesy ;
illustrated by Joe Lanzisero.
—1st ed.   p. cm.
Summary: Just before a big concert "Meowstro" Leopold von Kittenkatt
asks each of his musicians if they have seen his baton, then must
come up with a different way to lead his all-cat orchestra.
ISBN 978-1-4231-4583-7
[1. Stories in rhyme. 2. Lost and found possessions—Fiction. 3. Musicians—
Fiction. 4. Orchestra—Fiction. 5. Cats—Fiction.] I. Lanzisero, Joe, ill. II. Title.
PZ8.3.H4182Cat 2013
[E]—dc23 2012004539

To Vicki,
your love and support mean a lot
to this ol' mouser
—Scott

To Cora,
for your love, and for
encouraging my craziness
—Joe

Leopold von Kittenkatt

Is a conductor oh so grand.
He leads a special **orcatstra**,
With cats from every land.

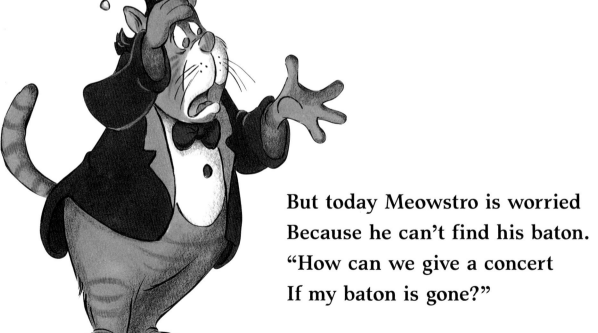

But today Meowstro is worried
Because he can't find his baton.
"How can we give a concert
If my baton is gone?"

"If I don't find it soon,
We're in trouble, and I mean it."
So he went to his **mewsicians**
To ask if they had seen it.

Meowstro went to Rico first,
Who plays the Mexican **guitar**.

Then to Sven, who comes from Sweden,
Where he's a **trombone** star.

He asked the Scottish **bagpiper**
From the MacCatty clan.

And the **taiko** drummer, Yoshi,
From the country of Japan.

He checked with Kenya's Jomo,
Who plays the **xylophone**.

With Swiss Miss Gabriele,
Whose **violin** has such nice tone.

But no one yet had seen the baton,
Or knew where it might be.
Meowstro felt he was headed for

a big

cat-tastrophe.

Next he spoke with Vladimir,
Who's from Russia, playing **cello**.

With Irish lassie, Erin,
Plucking **harp** so very mellow.

Then Fritz, playing "Oompaw-paw"
With his German **tuba**.

And Xavier, whose **conga drum**
Is all the rage in Cuba.

Next was Australia's Jirra,
With his **didgeridoo**'s calm drone.

And the U.S.A.'s "Mardi Cats,"
Led by Max on **saxophone**.

He spoke with China's Meow Li,
A **piano** virtuoso.

With Poland's Bronislaw,
Who plays a brand-new **oboe**.

He talked with Taj, from India.
His **pungi** can cause a

trance.

He followed up with Antoinette,
The **concertina** player from France.

When none of his **mewsicians**
Had seen his prized baton,
Meowstro became very sad:
The show would not go on.

Then something struck a chord
Like a note out of the blue.
He had a great idea
That showed him

what to do!

Once the audience was seated,
And the **orcatstra** was ready,
He stepped up to the podium,
Composed and calm and steady.

As he readied his **mewsicians**,
Meowstro knew he would not fail.
He led a **purrfect** concert
By conducting with . . .

Glossary

Bagpipe: A wind instrument consisting of a wind bag that has reed pipes attached to it. The player repeatedly fills the bag with air by blowing into a pipe, and also squeezes air from the bag, which passes through the reed pipes. Finger holes in one of the pipes let the bagpiper play the melody. The other pipes are called drones, and each makes one continuous tone.

Baton: A stick that an orchestra conductor uses to guide his or her musicians and help them keep time with the music.

Cello: This stringed instrument is the second-largest bass member of the violin family. The instrument stands upright with the player holding it between the knees. It has a fretless neck, four strings, and is played with a bow.

Concert Hall: A very large room in which an orchestra gives a musical performance.

Concertina: A small accordion-like instrument that is played by pushing its two sides together while pressing buttons on each end to create the melody.

Conductor: The leader of an orchestra, who stands in front of the musicians and directs them throughout the concert.

Conga Drum: A percussion instrument with a tall and tapered body that has a skin tightly stretched over one end. It is played by beating rhythms on it with one's hands.

Didgeridoo: Common among the Aborigines of Australia, this instrument is made from a long hollowed-out log. The player blows into it, and it makes a deep and low hypnotic drone.

Drum/Taiko: A percussion instrument that has a skin tightly stretched over one or both ends of a hollow cylinder. The drum is played by rhythmically hitting the skin with the hands or with drumsticks. *Taiko* is the Japanese word for "drum."

Guitar: A stringed instrument with a flat, hollow body and a long fretted neck. The guitar typically has six strings that the player strums or plucks with the fingers or a pick.

Harp: This stringed instrument consists of an upright triangle-shaped frame that has strings graduated in length stretched inside of it. The player leans the harp body against the right shoulder, reaches around each side of the frame with both hands, and plucks the strings with the fingers.

Maestro/*Meowstro*: This Italian word means "master." It is used to address conductors, as well as great composers, performers, and teachers of music.

Musician/*Mewsician*: A person—or cat—who plays a musical instrument.

Oboe: Made of a conical tube with various keys on it, this woodwind instrument has two reeds in the mouthpiece. The player blows through the double reed and makes different notes by pushing the keys.

Oompah-pah/Oom*paw-paw*: A repeated rhythmic bass sound typically made by a tuba, and common to German music.

Orchestra/Or*catstra*: An organized body of musicians that performs concerts together. A typical orchestra is made up of four sections: strings, brass, woodwinds, and percussion.

Piano: This stringed instrument has a keyboard with eighty-eight keys. The piano's sound is made when the player pushes each key down and it makes a felt-covered hammer strike a steel wire string. Each of the eighty-eight keys makes a different note.

Pungi: A wind instrument made from a gourd that has two wooden reed pipes inserted into it. One pipe has finger holes that the player uses to play the melody. The other pipe makes a droning sound. Snake charmers in India commonly play this instrument.

Saxophone: This wind instrument is made of a J-shaped brass tube with a flared end. The mouthpiece has a single reed that vibrates when the player blows into it, and different notes are created when the keys on the tube are pushed.

Trombone: A brass wind instrument that has a long metal tube with two turns in it and a flared bell-shaped end. It also has a U-shaped slide that the player moves back and forth while he or she blows into the mouthpiece. Moving the slide is how the instrument makes different notes.

Tuba: A large brass wind instrument made of an oval-shaped tube that has a large bell-like opening. The player blows into its cup-shaped mouthpiece and changes the notes by pressing valves positioned on the tube. The tuba has the lowest pitch of all the brass instruments.

Violin: This stringed instrument has a shallow wooden body, a fretless neck, and a head with pegs to tune its four strings. The player holds the violin out straight with its base positioned below the left side of the jaw. While fingering the neck with the left hand, the violinist moves a bow across the strings with the right hand.

Virtuoso: A very talented performer who shows great technical skill and mastery of their instrument.

Xylophone: This percussion instrument has a set of tuned wooden bars laid side by side from the shortest to the longest. The player uses two wooden mallets to strike the bars, which are tuned to produce the musical scale.

THE END